The Stallion
With a
Dream!

Cynthia Hickey

ISBN: 978-1-959788-21-8

Dedicated to Trinity. You're a beast!

Trin thought he was the fastest horse in the west. All he needed was the chance to prove it to everyone else.

"There is a big race coming up and I'm going to win it," he said.

"The only race I know about," his friend, Rupert the buzzard, said. "Is very, very far away and you are a very, very young horse."

"I'm also very fast. Watch me go!"

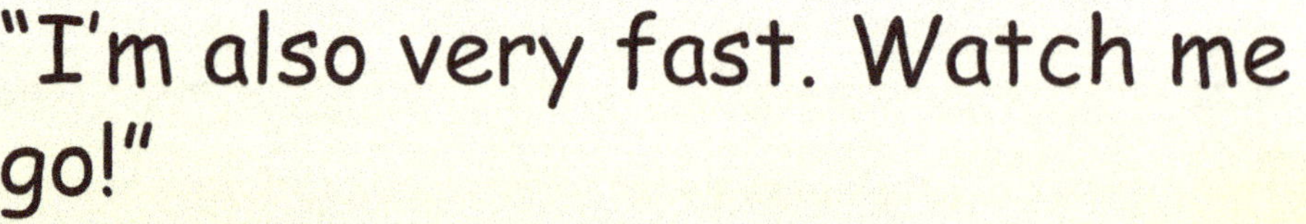

Rupert watched Trin gallop back and forth in front of him. "You aren't as fast as a full grown horse, yet."

"I'll be bigger by the time I reach the race. Watch me and see."

So, off Trin went.

The desert was much bigger the farther he got from the ranch. But the sights to see were beautiful!

Tall cactus, red rocks, and lots of sand. The desert was pretty, but Trin wanted the green grasses of race land.

So, he kept running and running and running.

Slowly, the scenery started to change, and he saw other horses.

"Hello. My name is cloud. Where are you going so fast?"

"My name is Trin and I'm going to win a big race."

"Dream big, little horse," a black horse
said. "We'll be rooting for you. Be careful
of the Phantom horse. Some say he will
take away your dream."

"Thank you." Trin trotted away. He had
high hopes of winning. Nothing would take
away his dream.

Trin had never heard of a phantom horse before, but if one truly lived, it would be in the dark forest.

Trin wasn't sure about entering the forest alone.

"Hello?"

When no one answered, Trin went further into the dark woods.

A storm rumbled with thunder and lightning when Trin left the forest. The loud noise and bright light frightened him. He ran faster.

He stopped when he spotted his friend. "Rupert, what are you doing here?"

"I've been following you, silly horse. A young horse should not travel alone," Rupert said.

So, Rupert went wherever Trin went. When Rupert got tired of flying, he simply...

rode on Trin's back. Trin never got tired of running. He wanted to win this race bad enough to never stop running.

He ran through bright green meadows next to blue lakes.

Days passed into weeks and weeks into months, and still Trin ran on. As he ran, he grew bigger and stronger.

Even Rupert had stopped saying that Trin didn't have a chance to win the race.

Then one day, they entered a scary forest full of strange lights.

And the phantom horse.

"Why are you here, little horse? This is my forest."

"I'm on my way to win a race."

"You're too young. Too small. Go home."

"I'm growing bigger and stronger every day. You wait and see. I'll be winning a wreath for coming in first place. You'll see."

Nothing would stop him. He'd come too far to turn back.

"Stay here until I return," Rupert said. "I want to see how much farther we have to go."

When Rupert returned he let Trin know that the horse racing stables were just over the next hill.

Trin got so excited, he galloped away.
Right over the hill, just as Rupert had said,
was the horse stables.

Trin gave his name at the door and settled into a stall to get a good night's rest. The big race was tomorrow.

"Good luck," Rupert said.

Trin's jockey wore purple. They were in last place for a long time, then Trin remembered all the hard work and running.

So, he ran faster, just as he'd practiced.

and faster until he won.
Trin had fulfilled his dream
and won the big race by
never giving up.

Trin got to wear the winner's wreath.
He'd never been so happy before.

"Happy Dreaming and never give up," he
told everyone. He was already looking
forward to the next race.

9 781959 788218